This book belongs to

_____

For Paul, Adrian, and Charlotte. With all my love.

-SG

I dedicate this book to those who have shared the lights of Channukah with me, and who have shared the warmth of the candles and of life with me over the years: My parents, Jodi and Frank, and my brother, Brent, who continue to shine their love on me everyday. My loved ones whose lights still shine brightly inside my heart, my I-Yai, Poppy, and Liz. All of my colleagues and friends, as well as my mentor and rabbi, M. Bruce Lustig, for all that he teaches me at Washington Hebrew Congregation. May all of us continue to celebrate this and all holidays together, and may we go from strength to strength.

-RABBI JOUI HESSEL

THE HANUKKAH FAMILY TREASURY

THE HANUKKAH
FAMILY TREASURY

BY STEVEN ZORN AND RABBI JOUI HESSEL

Illustrated by Sarah Gibb

COURAGE BOOKS

AN IMPRINT OF RUNNING PRESS
PHILADELPHIA • LONDON

© 2004 by Running Press
Illustrations © 2004 by Sarah Gibb
All rights reserved under the Pan-American and International Copyright Conventions.

Printed in China.

*This book may not be reproduced in whole or in part, in any form or by any means,
electronic or mechanical, including photocopying, recording, or by any information storage and
retrieval system now known or hereafter invented, without written permission from the publisher.*

9   8   7   6   5   4   3   2   1

Digit on the right indicates the number of this printing

Library of Congress Control Number: 2002115121

ISBN 0-7624-0776-X

Designed by Gwen Galeone
Illustrated by Sarah Gibb
Edited by Andra Serlin
Text written by Steven Zorn and Rabbi Joui Hessel
Typography: Plantin and Bembo

This book may be ordered by mail from the publisher.
But try your bookstore first!

Published by Courage Books, an imprint of
Running Press Book Publishers
125 South Twenty-second Street
Philadelphia, Pennsylvania 19103-4399

Visit us on the web!
www.runningpress.com

Contents

Introduction . . .8

Judah and the Maccabees . . .10

The Maccabees at War . . .14

Judah Maccabee
(FROM 1 MACCABEES 3: 3–9) . . .18

Rededicating the Temple
(from 1 Maccabees 4: 36–59) . . .20

Judith: A Hanukkah Heroine . . .24

The Banner of the Jew
by Emma Lazarus . . .32

Hanukkah Blessings . . .34

The Menorah . . .36

Make Your Own Hanukkah Candles . . .38

The Dreidel . . .40

Recipes . . .42

Songs . . .44

Introduction

WITH THE GLOW OF EACH CANDLE, THE MIRACLE OF HANUKKAH COMES TO LIFE. BUT HANUKKAH IS MORE THAN JUST A HOLIDAY OF LIGHTS. IT IS A CELEBRATION OF JEWISH FAITH IN THE FACE OF ADVERSITY AND A REMINDER OF HOW PRECIOUS OUR FREEDOM IS.

The history of Hanukkah began twenty-three centuries ago with the ancient Jews and their struggle to practice their religion freely under Greek rule. Brave Jewish people fought wars and withstood tortures, armed with only one true weapon: their faith. Upon winning back their holy Temple in Jerusalem, the Jews found there was only enough oil to keep the eternal lamp—the lamp which guards the Torah, the Jewish holy book, and symbolizes God's neverending presence in our lives—lit for one night. A miracle occurred when the candles continued to burn for more than a week, long enough for more oil to be made.

While the word Hanukkah has come to mean "dedication," the celebration of the holiday is not only in honor of the dedication of Temple, but also an acknowledgement of the dedication it took for the Jewish people to keep their faith in trying times.

Today, the miracle that allowed a day's worth of oil to burn for eight remains just as remarkable. The struggles and triumphs of a people are remembered and the light shines just as bright, as people celebrate the miracle of Hanukkah in their own homes.

THE STORY OF
JUDAH AND THE MACCABEES

The story of the miracle of Hanukkah begins almost two thousand three hundred years ago in days when most of the Middle East was under the influence of the Greek government.

At first, that didn't seem so bad. The Greeks developed gorgeous architecture and art, they appreciated philosophy and literature, and they enjoyed sports and leisure.

Because the Greeks had so much to offer, most countries in the Middle East gladly adopted their ways. Soon the people of these countries forgot the ways of their ancestors. They began to dress like the Greeks, build their buildings in the style of the Greeks, speak the Greek language, and even worship the Greek gods. The hodgepodge of cultures blended together with the Greek culture was called Hellenism, after *Hellas*, the Greek word for Greece.

In Judea, a small and poor strip of land that linked Asia and Africa, the Jews weren't entirely happy about Hellenism. While they appreciated many of the benefits the Greeks had brought, there were some things that they couldn't accept. They wouldn't give up their ancient rituals and they refused to bow down to the idols of the Greeks.

To the Hellenistic leaders of Judea, the Jews were a peculiar and stubborn people, but they paid their taxes and they seemed harmless enough. They were allowed to go about their business and worship their nameless, faceless God. They were allowed their holy Temple and their holy city of Jerusalem. They were allowed to study the Torah and to live as their ancestors had always lived.

But then, in the year 175 B.C.E. (Before the Common Era), a new dynasty came to power. On its throne sat the Syrian monarch Antiochus Epiphanes, known as Antiochus IV. He wanted everyone under his rule to be Greek in every way. If they refused, they would be killed. Some Jews gave in. Others didn't, and many died for their beliefs.

For months, the people of Modi'in, a village just west of Jerusalem, had been talking about the problems the Greeks were causing. Jews in neighboring towns were being forced to eat unkosher animals or were made to convert under threat of death. Much blood was spilled; the old ways were being destroyed. The Jewish people were in danger of being wiped out entirely.

One day a traveler passed through Modi'in and spoke to Mattathias, an old Jewish priest who lived in the village with his sons.

"Did you hear what happened in Jerusalem?" the traveler asked Mattathias.

"No. But I'll bet it's more trouble," replied the priest.

"It's terrible, terrible news." replied the traveler. "Elazar, a priest like yourself, is dead— killed by the Greeks at the age of ninety."

"Tell me what happened," said Mattathias, very concerned.

"The Greek governor demanded that a pig be sacrificed and eaten to honor the king and the Greek gods. When Elazar refused, the governor tried to strike a bargain with him."

"A bargain? What sort of bargain?" asked Mattathias.

"The governor told Elazar that he could take a kosher animal, secretly slaughter it according to Jewish law, and then eat it before the Jews of Jerusalem, making them think that he was eating pork," replied the traveler.

"Asking a priest to deceive his own people into abandoning their ways? This is terrible!" exclaimed Mattathias, his anger rising. "No priest would ever do such a thing."

"Of course not," the traveler agreed. "And because he refused, the Greek soldiers beat him to death."

This news deeply troubled Mattathias. Soon, news came that the once great city of Jerusalem had become a haven for thieves and killers. The most holy Temple had become a shrine to the Greek god Zeus; its altar defiled with sacrifices of unholy animals. This place that once held such joy for the Jews was now ruined. The Jewish residents of Jerusalem had all fled. The glory of the city was no more. There seemed no end to the troubles caused by Antiochus. Mattathias knew that it was only a matter of time before soldiers paid Modi'in a visit. What would he and the villagers do then?

In 167 B.C.E., the dreaded day arrived when the forces of King Antiochus rode into town. An officer approached Mattathias at a public gathering and said to him, "You are a leader of your people and the father of five fine sons. Be the first to follow the king's commands and others will follow you."

"What is it you ask of me and of my people?" asked Mattathias.

"We ask only a sacrifice to the glory of the gods and the glory of Antiochus, who is like a god. Others of your people have offered similar sacrifices and have been rewarded with wealth and honor. You'll be granted these things, too, if you offer up a pig upon the altar."

"To do what you ask would be to forsake my religion and my ancestors. I would be turning my back on God. I can never do this thing," swore Mattathias, seething with rage.

No sooner had Mattathias finished speaking than one of the townspeople of Modi'in, a Jew, brought forward a pig for sacrifice.

When Mattathias saw this, he could no longer control his fury. He slew the man right there on the altar. Then he killed the officer.

Everyone was stunned. Mattathias knew

what to do next. Meanwhile, the king's forces rallied nearby. The townsfolk of Modi'in were now considered rebels and outlaws.

"Come out from where you're hiding," urged the soldiers. "Do what the king commands, and you will live."

But the townsfolk kept silent so as not to reveal their hiding places. It was Sabbath and they had agreed that they would not fight the soldiers, even if attacked. "Let us all die innocent, and heaven and earth will testify that we are killed unjustly."

that now was the time for action. He shouted in a voice loud and strong, "Everyone who is zealous for the law and supports the covenant with God come out with me!"

And he and his sons and many of their friends fled to the hills, leaving behind all they had.

Others ran off to seek shelter in the wilderness below. They hid there, planning

The soldiers hunted them down like wild animals and killed them all—including women and children.

When news of this horror spread, many Jews felt that they had no choice but to convert to the pagan religion. But not everyone converted. Some took action, and their action changed history. The tide would soon turn against King Antiochus.

THE MACCABEES AT WAR

When Mattathias, his five sons, and their other allies in the mountains learned how the army of Antiochus had senselessly slaughtered innocent people, it hardened their resolve. They knew they had no choice but to fight.

They organized an army, and soon Jews who were fleeing the Greeks from other towns came and joined them. The Jews learned to be great warriors. Even though their numbers were small and the Greeks outnumbered them three to one, they swept into towns to tear down altars set up by the Greeks for their idol worship.

Years went by, and Mattathias grew old.

Though there were many skirmishes, the great battle—the fight to regain the Temple in Jerusalem and make it holy again—was yet to be fought. Before Mattathias died he appointed his third son, Judah, to command the army and deliver the Jews to victory.

Judah was a smart, tough man who was unafraid to use force. He became known as Maccabee, which means "the hammer." The

civilian army he trained called themselves Maccabees. The Syrians would soon learn that this rag-tag army of teachers and farmers and weavers was a force to contend with.

What the Maccabees lacked in numbers and strength, they made up for in cunning and motivation. The Syrian army fought for money or because it was the king's command. The Maccabees fought for their God, their beliefs, and their freedom to worship freely.

Judah Maccabee was a master of guerilla warfare. He and his men would swoop down under cover of night and set fire to the camps of enemy soldiers. No one knew when or where he would attack. Judah knew all the caves and rock outcroppings where he and his troops could hide. He knew where to place himself for the best vantage point, and he knew mountain passes which the Syrians would likely choose. His knowledge of the land made it easy for him and his army to move at a moment's notice and to strike seemingly from out of nowhere. He began to be taken seriously.

Soon, he became such a threat that armies were organized against him. His first battle was against General Appolonius, who underestimated the Maccabee forces. The general's forces turned tail and fled when Judah killed Appolonius. That day, the Maccabees gathered up the armor and weapons of the defeated army to use as their own. Judah took the general's sword and used it in battles for the rest of his life.

Hearing about the defeat of Appolonius, General Seron of the Syrian army began planning his own attack. Seron thought he would be able to defeat the Maccabees and win honor for himself. His army was twice the size of Appolonius's but he, too, underestimated his opponent. Seron's army had to move through a small pass in the mountains in order to get to Judah's men. But Judah's small group was ready for him. They got to the pass first, and when the army approached, the Maccabees were ready with sword in hand. They killed eight hundred of Seron's men. The rest fled. Victory, again, went to the Maccabees.

And on it went. With each victory, more people came to join the cause of the Maccabees. Their ranks swelled, but never approached the numbers of the men who swore to stop them. Judah's success lay not with strength, but with strategy. He had men hiding everywhere, spying on their enemies and ready to report back what they heard so the Maccabees could plan with foresight.

Two generals named Gorgias and Nicanor tried to beat the Maccabees at their own game by planning surprise attacks. Gorgias' army set up camp at a place in the mountains called Emmaus. Then he took half of his men out looking for the hidden camp of the Maccabees. After some searching, they thought they found it. The campfires were lit, but no one was there. It looked as if the Maccabees had abandoned the camp in a hurry. Gorgias believed that he and his fearsome army must have frightened them off. He left there feeling flush with victory.

Gorgias was wrong. While he and his men were looking for the Maccabee camp, Judah and his men were attacking Gorgias's camp and the rest of his army, who were unprepared for the assault. The Maccabees killed them or ran them off. Then they burned their tents and supplies and drove off their animals. When Gorgias returned and saw what had happened, he was stunned. He and his army fled in defeat.

For three difficult years the Maccabees fought the Syrian army, finally making their way into the city of Jerusalem to reclaim the Holy Temple. And when they arrived there, they faced what might have been their hardest work of all: cleaning the Temple up and making it holy once again.

Judah saw that one of the Jews' most sacred places lay in ruins. The altar had been destroyed, and unclean animals had been sacrificed upon the place where it once stood. Statues of Greek gods towered over the cluttered mess. All that was beautiful or useful had been broken or stolen. When the Jews saw this, they wept and prayed. Then they went to work.

month of the Jewish calendar, the month known as *Kislev*, the temple was ready. The year was 164 B.C.E. The Maccabees dedicated the Temple and lit the *Ner Tamid*, the Eternal Light. There was only one problem. Most of the oil in the Temple had been tainted. The Maccabees found just one sealed flask that could be used, but it had only enough oil to last for a single day. It would take

Some people swept out the filth and the shards of shattered pottery, while others pushed out the statues. Together they tore down the crumbled, polluted altar and built a clean, new one out of whole stones, according to ancient law. Potters and metalworkers busied themselves making candlesticks, incense burners, and pots for sacred oil. Young children helped pull weeds and plant flowers in the outside courtyard. Walls and floors were scrubbed inside and out. Old women sewed curtains to adorn the windows. The smell of fresh bread perfumed the air and drove out the mustiness.

Finally, on the twenty-fifth day of the ninth

more than a week to make more oil for the Eternal Light.

Miraculously the oil burned for eight days, long enough for more oil to be made. This was a small but significant miracle that illuminated the greater miracle of the Maccabees' victory over their enemies. What is perhaps the greatest miracle of all is that those lights are still burning just as brightly today as we celebrate Hanukkah in our own homes. The word Hanukkah has come to mean "dedication"—not just the dedication of the Holy Temple, but the dedication it took the Maccabees to persevere in very dangerous and difficult times.

JUDAH MACCABEE

from 1 Maccabees 3: 3–9

While the Books of the Maccabees tell a historically
accurate version of the story of Hanukkah, the books are
part of the *Apocrypha*, a Greek history, and are not
found in the Hebrew Bible.

So he gat his people great honour, and put on a breastplate
as a giant, and girt his warlike harness about him, and he made
battles, protecting the host with his sword.

In his acts he was like a lion, and like a lion's whelp
roaring for his prey.

For he pursued the wicked, and sought them out, and burnt up
those that vexed his people.

Wherefore the wicked shrunk for fear of him, and all the
workers of iniquity were troubled, because salvation prospered
in his hand.

He grieved also many kings, and made Jacob glad with his
acts, and his memorial is blessed for ever.

Moreover he went through the cities of Judah, destroying the
ungodly out of them, and turning away wrath from Israel:

So that he was renowned unto the utmost part of the earth . . .

REDEDICATING THE TEMPLE

from 1 Maccabees 4: 36–59

Then said Judah and his brethren, Behold, our enemies are discomfited: let us go up to cleanse and dedicate the sanctuary.

Upon this all the host assembled themselves together, and went up into mount Zion.

And when they saw the sanctuary desolate, and the altar profaned, and the gates burned up, and shrubs growing in the courts as in a forest, or in one of the mountains, yea, and the priests' chambers pulled down;

They rent their clothes, and made great lamentation, and cast ashes upon their heads,

And fell down flat to the ground upon their faces, and blew an alarm with the trumpets, and cried toward heaven.

Then Judah appointed certain men to fight against those that were in the fortress, until he had cleansed the sanctuary.

So he chose priests of blameless conversation, such as had pleasure in the law:

Who cleansed the sanctuary, and bare out the defiled stones into an unclean place.

And when as they consulted what to do with the altar of burnt offerings, which was profaned;

They thought it best to pull it down, lest it should be a reproach to them, because the heathen had defiled it: wherefore they pulled it down,

And laid up the stones in the mountain of the temple in a convenient place, until there should come a prophet to shew what should be done with them.

Then they took whole stones according to the law, and built a new altar according to the former;

And made up the sanctuary, and the things that were within the temple, and hallowed the courts.

They made also new holy vessels, and into the temple they brought the candlestick, and the altar of burnt offerings, and of incense, and the table.

And upon the altar they burned incense, and the lamps that
were upon the candlestick they lighted, that they might give
light in the temple.

Furthermore they set the loaves upon the table, and spread
out the veils, and finished all the works which they had begun
to make.

Now on the five and twentieth day of the ninth month, which
is called the month *Kislev*, in the hundred forty and eighth
year, they rose up betimes in the morning,

And offered sacrifice according to the law upon the new altar
of burnt offerings, which they had made.

Look, at what time and what day the heathen had profaned it,
even in that was it dedicated with songs, and citterns, and
harps, and cymbals.

Then all the people fell upon their faces, worshipping and praising the God of heaven, who had given them good success.

And so they kept the dedication of the altar eight days and offered burnt offerings with gladness, and sacrificed the sacrifice of deliverance and praise.

They decked also the forefront of the temple with crowns of gold, and with shields; and the gates and the chambers they renewed, and hanged doors upon them.

Thus was there very great gladness among the people, for that the reproach of the heathen was put away.

Moreover Judah and his brethren with the whole congregation of Israel ordained, that the days of the dedication of the altar should be kept in their season from year to year by the space of eight days, from the five and twentieth day of the month *Kislev*, with mirth and gladness.

JUDITH: A HANUKKAH HEROINE

YOU KNOW THAT JUDAH MACCABEE WAS THE BRAVE HERO BEHIND THE HANUKKAH STORY. BUT THERE'S ANOTHER HERO—A HEROINE—WHO DELIVERED HER PEOPLE FROM CONQUERING FORCES. SHE WAS JUST AS VALIANT AS JUDAH AND EVEN HAD A SIMILAR NAME. SHE WAS CALLED JUDITH.

Judith lived in different times than Judah Maccabee, but her story has been linked to the festival of Hanukkah. This is because Hanukkah is a celebration of Jewish faith in the face of trouble. Judith's times were grim, indeed; her people were on the verge of destruction. But her faith never wavered, not even for an instant.

In Judith's time, the king of Assyria grew very powerful. In fact, he grew so powerful that he believed he could rule the world. Even more, he believed that everyone on earth should worship him as a god. So he sent Holofernes, the chief captain of his army, out to conquer those cities and nations that refused to heed the king's orders.

Holofernes commanded a huge and powerful army. It swept through the land, leveling cities like a sword through tall grass. Nations fell one after another as Holofernes cut his bloody path. And where was he heading? To Judea and the holy city of Jerusalem. He had heard about the Jews and their stubbornness. He swore he would be the one to change their faith—or to destroy them in the process.

Between Holofernes's army and Judea lay hill country. The villagers nestled in these hills fortified themselves as best they could against the

approaching army. They reaped their fields and stored their grain; the people headed for the mountaintops so they could see when the distant army drew near. Then they could decide whether to fight or to run.

Holofernes and his army pressed on through town after town, inching closer to Judea. They made it as far as Bethulia, the city right next to Judea. Here the army met its first real challenge. The mountains made Bethulia a natural fortress that defied invasion. Narrow passes allowed only two soldiers to squeeze through at a time. There was no way to storm the city.

As the army planned their strategy in the mountains, one of Holofernes's advisors said to him, "Commander, I have heard that the Jews of Bethulia worship a powerful God. This God protects them so long as they keep their holy laws. And while they keep those laws, we will not be able to take the city."

"Nonsense!" answered Holofernes. "These people are weak. Their God shall not deliver them. The only god is our king, who has sent us on this mission. To speak of this Jewish God the way you do is treason. If you trust in this God so much, then I'll send you to Bethulia. If the people there don't destroy you as an enemy, then I will when I conquer the city."

The advisor was sent off to Bethulia, where his fate was uncertain.

The people of Bethulia took him in, and he told them what had happened. He also warned them that Holofernes's army numbered more than thirteen thousand soldiers, and they were planning an attack.

In the tense days that followed, the worried

folk of Bethulia prayed that their God wouldn't abandon them. Meanwhile, the army closed off the city, allowing no one in or out, hoping to starve the villagers into surrendering. Then the situation got worse. The soldiers discovered the hidden stream that carried Bethulia's only supply of fresh water, and stopped it, cutting off the people's drinking water. Any pot or pitcher or bucket of water became precious beyond measure. All the Assyrian army had to do was wait until all the water was gone. Thirty-four days passed, and Bethulia began to wither and die.

Inside the town, the Jews continued to pray. But weakened by hunger and thirst, they begged their mayor to surrender to the Assyrians. The mayor said to them, "Let us wait and pray for five more days. Surely in five days, God will help us. If God doesn't, then we'll surrender."

Judith, a widow in the city, heard these words and scolded the mayor. "It is not fair to put God to the test," she said. "You don't know God's will, and you can't make a bargain with God. God has the power to save us or destroy us. This five day deadline you've given God means nothing."

"Well, then, what do you suggest, Judith?" asked the mayor.

"This is a time for action," Judith replied. "I have a plan in mind. In those five days that you mentioned, I'll save the city—if that's God's will. Please don't ask me any questions, but just do as I ask."

Judith was a pious and well-respected woman. Her husband had died more than three years earlier, leaving her a young widow who had to learn to depend on herself. She was smart and attractive, wealthy, and—as we shall see—brave and clever.

The mayor, while puzzled by Judith's request, had complete faith in her. He agreed to help her, whatever it was she planned to do—without asking a single question.

Judith went back to her home to prepare herself. Widows in those days wore very simple, drab clothing. But this night things would be different. After praying for strength and the safety of her people, Judith shed her clothes and bathed. She perfumed her body and her hair. Then she went through the fine she had kept from her married days. She chose something elegant and attractive, and selected fine earrings and chains and bracelets to flatter herself even more.

Judith asked her maid to gather bottles of fine wine, wheels of cheese, some oil, lumps of figs, fine bread, and other delicacies. These things were difficult to find because even stale bread was growing scarce in the city. Then Judith and her maid went to the gates of Bethulia. On their way, people were amazed at how beautiful she looked. She had not looked this way since the death of her husband. The mayor met her at the city gate. He wanted to ask her what she was up to, but he had promised that he wouldn't. So he ordered that the gates be opened and that Judith and her maid be allowed to pass through.

The mayor and others from the city watched as Judith and her maid traveled down the mountain into the valley, and finally disappeared from site.

A while later, the guards of the Assyrian army couldn't believe what they were seeing. Out of the darkness came the vision of a woman. She was splendidly dressed and her servant accompanied her. It was a strange thing to see in these war-weary times.

As Judith grew nearer, the guards stopped her. "Who are you?" they demanded. "Where do you come from and where are you going?"

"I am a woman of the Hebrews," said Judith, without hesitation, without fear. "I have fled from them because you are sure to kill them all."

"Then why do you come to us?" asked the guards.

"I want to be a part of the winning side," answered Judith. "I'd like to meet with your commander, Holofernes. My people have no chance, but I can show Holofernes how to conquer the Hebrews without losing any of his men."

"Well, then," said the guards, "we'll take you to see him."

Judith and her maid were brought to the tent of Holofernes, accompanied by a hundred soldiers who marveled at her beauty. The great commander invited her to enter. She went in, very timidly, with her head bowed low to show him great respect.

"Fear not," said Holofernes. "I will not harm anyone who is willing to serve the king of Assyria, the one true lord. The Hebrew people are in trouble only because they refuse to accept this."

Judith said to him, "The men of my city spoke with the servant that you banished from your army and sent to Bethulia. He told us how powerful your forces are. But even if you don't kill us with your swords, Bethulia is slowly dying from hunger and thirst because your army won't let food or water into the city. That is why I couldn't stay there. I don't want to die like that. I want to live."

Holofernes was impressed by Judith. He had no reason to suspect that she was getting ready to deceive him.

Judith continued her story. "What your servant told you about the Hebrew God was correct. The Jews cannot be defeated while their

God protects them. But I know that the Jews are about to commit a sin before God, and God will turn against them. Hunger will soon force them to eat unclean animals and consume sacred wine and oil. That will anger their God. Then your army will be able to attack and destroy the Jews of Bethulia."

This news was encouraging to Holofernes. Soon his long wait would be over. His army could sweep through Bethulia and then go on to conquer Judea for the glory of his king.

"Let me remain here," said Judith. "At night I will go out into the wilderness with my servant and I'll pray to my God. God will tell me when my people have committed their sins. When they do, I'll let you know. Then I'll lead you and your army to victory."

Holofernes replied, "Judith, this is a good plan. You may stay here in safety for as long as you need. If you bring us this victory, you'll be renowned throughout the world."

Holofernes made sure that a comfortable tent was set up for Judith and her servant. They were treated like royalty and given every comfort. Holofernes enjoyed Judith's company. They shared

meals together and delightful conversation. Judith impressed him with her intelligence and sense of humor.

Each night for three nights, Judith would leave the camp and go into the wilderness to pray. But she didn't pray to find out when her people would sin. She prayed that God would rescue her people and that Holofernes would

fall for her trick. So far it was working according to her plan.

By the fourth night, Judith had fully won the trust of Holofernes. Now it was time for her to act. At dinner, she had her servant bring the cheeses, wines, and other delicacies that she had packed when she left Bethulia. Once her servant brought them, Judith dismissed her. Holofernes asked his servants to leave as well. Now Judith and Holofernes were dining alone.

Judith placed the cheese on the table and poured Holofernes a large cup of wine. "These are fine foods of my people," said Judith, "I'd be honored if you would have some."

Holofernes sampled the salty cheese and liked it. But the salt made him thirsty, so he sipped the wine. He enjoyed that, too. Judith kept his wine cup filled, and kept the salty food coming so Holofernes would desire even more wine. Judith delighted him with her company and he didn't realize how much he was drinking. The hours slipped by and the wine flowed like water. Finally, Holofernes had had enough to drink. In fact, he had too much. Judith helped him to his bed, where he fell deeply asleep.

This was the moment Judith had been waiting for. The great commander was completely helpless—his guards and servants

had been sent away. Seeing her chance, Judith pulled Holofernes's sword from the wall and, praying for strength, swung it down hard. In one swift move, she cut off Holofernes's head. She gathered it into a sack and left the tent.

The hour was late. Most soldiers slept. Judith went to collect her maid. The two women walked casually out of the camp carrying the sack with Holofernes's head. By now the guards were used to seeing them leave the camp at night and didn't stop them. No one suspected a thing.

Judith and her servant headed back to Bethulia with their prize. The watchman at the city gates called the mayor and the town elders to let them know that Judith had returned. They lit a fire to welcome her and to see her better. A crowd gathered. Everyone wanted to know what had happened these past four days.

Judith took the head out of the bag and showed them. "Behold the head of Holofernes!" she shouted victoriously. "The Lord has destroyed the chief captain of the Assyrian army by the hand of a woman!"

A huge cheer arose from the people of Bethulia. They knew they were saved. But they still had work to do.

"Listen," said Judith. "Tomorrow morning, we need to take up our weapons and head toward the Assyrian camp. When the soldiers see us coming, they'll rush to tell Holofernes. Then they'll discover that he is dead. Without his leadership, fear will overcome them and they'll flee. Bethulia, Judea, and the Jewish people will be spared."

And that is exactly what happened. A nation was saved by the actions of one brave woman.

THE BANNER OF THE JEW

by Emma Lazarus

EMMA LAZARUS (1849-1887) IS BEST REMEMBERED FOR HER SONNET, "The New Colossus," WHOSE WORDS, "GIVE ME YOUR TIRED, YOUR POOR, YOUR HUDDLED MASSES YEARNING TO BREATHE FREE..." ARE INSCRIBED ON THE PEDESTAL OF THE STATUE OF LIBERTY. "The Banner of the Jew," PUBLISHED IN 1882 CELEBRATES THE VICTORY OF THE HEROIC MACCABEES.

Wake, Israel, wake! Recall to-day
The glorious Maccabean rage,
The sire heroic, hoary-gray,
His five-fold lion-lineage:
The Wise, the Elect, the Help-of-God,
The Burst-of-Spring, the Avenging Rod.

From Mizpeh's mountain-ridge they saw
Jerusalem's empty streets, her shrine
Laid waste where Greeks profaned the Law,
With idol and with pagan sign.
Mourners in tattered black were there,
With ashes sprinkled on their hair.

Then from the stony peak there rang
A blast to ope the graves: down poured
The Maccabean clan, who sang
Their battle-anthem to the Lord.
Five heroes lead, and following, see,
Ten thousand rush to victory!

Oh for Jerusalem's trumpet now,

To blow a blast of shattering power,

To wake the sleepers high and low,

And rouse them to the urgent hour!

No hand for vengeance--but to save,

A million naked swords should wave.

Oh deem not dead that martial fire,

Say not the mystic flame is spent!

With Moses' law and David's lyre,

Your ancient strength remains unbent.

Let but an Ezra rise anew,

To lift the BANNER OF THE JEW!

A rag, a mock at first--erelong,

When men have bled and women wept,

To guard its precious folds from wrong,

Even they who shrunk, even they who slept,

Shall leap to bless it, and to save.

Strike! for the brave revere the brave!

Hanukkah Blessings

THE FIRST TWO BLESSINGS ARE READ EVERY NIGHT OF HANUKKAH
AFTER THE *SHAMASH* IS LIT, BUT BEFORE LIGHTING THE OTHER CANDLES.

 First Blessing

Barukh atah Adonai, Elohaynu melekh ha-olam

Asher kidishanu b'mitzvo-tav

Vi-tzivahnu le-hadlikh ner shel Hanukkah

Praised are You, Adonai, our God,

Ruler of the universe, Who has made us holy thorough

God's commandments and commanded us to

kindle the Hanukkah lights.

Second Blessing

Barukh atah Adonai, Elohaynu melekh ha-olam
She-asah nisim l'voteynu, ba-yamim ha-hem,
ba-zman ha-zeh

Praised are You, Adonai, our God,
Ruler of the Universe, Who performed miracles
for our ancestors in ancient times at this season.

 ## Third Blessing

Read the third blessing only
on the first night of Hanukkah.

Barukh atah Adonai, Elohaynu melekh ha-olam
She-hekhiyanu, v'kiyimanu, v'higiyanu
laz-man hazeh

Praised are You, Adonai, our God,
Ruler of the Universe, Who has kept us alive
and sustained us, and enabled us to reach this season.

THE MENORAH

A Menorah, the Hebrew word for "candelabrum," is a lamp of any kind. A *Chanukiyah* is the distinctive nine-branched shape that has become the symbol of Hanukkah. Eight candles represent the miracle of the oil that burned for eight days. The ninth candle, called the *shamash*, or "servant" is used to light the others, and is therefore set apart from the rest of the candles. Hanukkah candles are supposed to burn for at least a half hour and their light is to be enjoyed for its own sake—not to provide illumination for reading or other tasks. The individual candles should be spaced far enough apart so that each flame remains distinct when the *Chanukiyah* is seen from a distance. On Friday, the *Chanukiyah* should be lit 18 minutes before sundown, before the Sabbath candles are lit.

Place the candles into the menorah from right to left, but light the candles from left to right. Everyone in the family should help light the *Chanukiyah*. The joyful light of the *Chanukiyah* should be shared with neighbors, too. The perfect place for it is in a front window, traditionally to the left of the doorway upon entering the house.

Make Your Own Hanukkah Candles

Increase your Hanukkah fun by making your own candles. It is easy to do with wicks and sheets of beeswax sold in arts and crafts stores.

Your candles can be as tall or as wide as you wish—but just remember, you'll need forty-four of them to take you through all eight nights. Just remember: the only "rule" about Hanukkah candles is that they must burn for at least thirty minutes. Keeping your candles in the freezer will help them burn a little longer.

To make your candles, cut a length of wick slightly longer than the height you want your candle to be. Lay it on the edge of the beeswax sheet. Start rolling the wax around the wick like you're rolling up a little rug. The tighter you roll, the longer your candle will burn. When the candle is as wide as you want it to be, trim off the extra wax with a pair of scissors. Now repeat 43 more times and you'll be all set!

Most menorahs are made for tiny candles. If your homemade candles don't fit, don't worry. You can improvise your own *Chanukiyah*. Just use some melted wax to stick the candles onto a large plate or tray. You can stick the shamash onto the bottom of an inverted mug or cup to raise it above the other candles. It's not really a *Chanukiyah*, but it'll still be festive and fun—and isn't that the point?

Start rolling the wax around the wick like you're rolling up a little rug. The tighter you roll, the longer your candle will burn.

Heat the bottom of the candle and then flatten it on a plate to make it stand properly in your *Chanukiyah*.

THE DREIDEL

The dreidel's ancestor is a toy top that German boys and girls played with. The word "dreidel" is Yiddish for top. The Hebrew word is "sivivon."

Nun

Gimmel

Each side of the dreidel has a Hebrew letter: Each letter represents the first word in the sentence *"Nais gadol hayah sham"*, which means "A great miracle happened there." That miracle, of course, is the recapture of the Temple of Jerusalem by the Maccabees. In Israel, dreidels are a little different. Instead of ש for "sham" or "there", they have the letter פ, the initial of the word "poh", meaning "here", because that's where the miracle happened.

The letters on the dreidel have come to stand for other words, too. And these words form the basis of the dreidel game. In Yiddish, נ (nun) stands for *nicht*, which means "take nothing"; ג (gimel), stands for *ganz*, or "take all"; ה (heh), represents *halb* or "take half"; and ש (shin) means *shtell*, or "put in."

To play the game, every player is given an equal number of game pieces. You can use coins, candies, peanuts, or whatever you'd like. The object is to collect all the pieces. To start, everyone puts one piece into the center, or the pot. Players then take turns spinning the dreidel. If it lands on נ (nun), the spinner neither takes nor puts in any pieces. If a player spins ג (gimel), he or she takes everything in the pot. A ה (heh), means the spinner takes half. If there's an odd number of pieces in the pot, then the spinner takes half plus one. Rolling a ש (shin) means the spinner puts two pieces into the pot.

When the pot is empty, each player puts in a piece and the game continues. The game can often last quite a while. Some players play only until one participant loses all of his or her pieces. Then, the player with the most pieces is considered to be the winner.

Shin

Heh

Recipes

Hanukkah is a time of great feasting and merriment. Because of the holiday's connection with miraculous oil, Hanukkah foods are traditionally fried. Here are two favorite recipes.

LATKES

Ingredients:
5 medium potatoes
1 medium onion
1 egg
1 teaspoon salt
a dash of pepper
2 tablespoons flour
  or matzo meal
oil for frying

1. Peel the potatoes and onions, then grate them. The coarse side of the grater will make the latkes more crunchy; the fine side will make them creamier. It's your choice.

2. Add the egg, salt, pepper, and flour or matzo meal. Mix well.

3. Pour enough oil into a skillet to cover the bottom generously.

4. Heat the pan over medium heat. You'll know it's hot enough when a pinch of flour sizzles. Don't let the oil get so hot that it smokes.

5. Spoon the batter into the pan. The pancakes should be 3-4 inches across.

6. Fry the latkah until it is brown on one side, then flip it over and brown the other side.

7. Carefully lift the latkes out and drain them on paper towels.

8. Serve 'em up! Try them with apple sauce, sour cream, or grated cheese.

DOUGHNUTS

Doughnuts are a treat any time of year. At Hanukkah time in Israel, they serve jelly-filled doughnuts called *sufganiyot*. In Poland, yeast donuts are called *ponchiks*. The recipe here is faster than yeast doughnuts and easier than jelly doughnuts—but equally delicious.

Ingredients:

2 cups flour
2 teaspoons baking powder
1 teaspoon cinnamon
pinch salt
1 egg
1/2 cup sugar
1/2 cup milk
2 tablespoons melted butter or margarine
Oil for deep frying
Powdered sugar for sprinkling

1. In a large bowl, mix together the flour, baking powder, cinnamon and salt. Set aside.

2. In another bowl, beat the egg. Then slowly add the sugar, beating constantly.

3. Add the milk and melted butter.

4. Pour the wet ingredients into the dry ingredients. Mix well.

5. Roll the dough out onto a lightly floured board to a thickness of about a half inch. Use a glass to cut out two- or three-inch diameter circles. Use a knife or a smaller glass to cut out the center of the circles. (You can fry these cut-outs separately, or re-roll them into more doughnuts.)

6. In a heavy, deep pot, heat four or five inches of oil over medium heat. You'll know it's ready when a pinch of the dough sizzles and browns quickly. If the oil smokes, it's too hot.

7. Put the doughnuts in a few at a time. Don't crowd them or they won't cook fast enough and they'll be greasy. They should take two to three minutes per side to reach a nice golden color.

8. As they come out, drain them on paper towels.

9. Sprinkle with powdered sugar just before serving.

My Dreidle

I have a little dreidle
I made it out of clay
And when it's dry and ready
Then dreidle I shall play.

O dreidle, dreidle, dreidle
I made it out of clay
O dreidle, dreidle, dreidle
Now dreidle I shall play

It has a lovely body
With legs so short and thin
And when it is all tired
It drops and then I win.

O dreidle, dreidle, dreidle
I made it out of clay
O dreidle, dreidle, dreidle
Now dreidle I shall play.

My dreidle's always playful
It loves to dance and spin
A happy game of dreidle
Come play, now let's begin.

O dreidle, dreidle, dreidle
I made it out of clay
O dreidle, dreidle, dreidle
Now dreidle I shall play.

Ma'oz Tzur
(Rock of Ages)

**This song was composed in Europe by a man named Mordechai,
sometime in the twelfth or thirteenth century. Little is known about him.**

Ma'oz Tzur y'shu-a-ti
L'kha na-eh lisha-bay-akh
Ti-kon beit t-fila-ti
V'sham to-da n'za-bay-akh
L-eit takhin mat-bay-akh
Mitzar ham'na-bay-akh
Az egmor b-shir miz-mor
chanukat hamiz-bay-akh

Rock of Ages, let our song
praise Your saving power.
You amidst our raging foes
were our sheltering tower.
Furious they assailed us
But Your arm availed us.
And Your word broke their sword
when our own strength failed us.

Mi Y'maleil (Who Can Retell?)

Mi y'ma-lel g'vu-rot Yisrael?
O tan-mi yim-ne?
Hen b'hol dor ya-kum ha-ge-bor
go el ha-am.
Sh'ma!
Ba-yamim ha-heim baz'man ha-zeh
Maccabi moshiya u-fodeh
Uv'yameinu kol am Yisrael
Yit'ached yakum l'hi-ga-el

* * *

Who can retell the things that befell them?
Who can count them?
In every age a hero or sage
came to our aid.
Hark!
In days of old in Israel's ancient land
Brave Maccabeus led his faithful band.
But now all Israel must as one arise,
Redeem itself through deed and sacrifice.